First American edition, 1989

Text copyright © 1989 by Grisewood & Dempsey Ltd.
Illustrations copyright © 1989 by Sarah Pooley
All rights reserved under International and Pan-American
Copyright Conventions. Published in the United States
by Random House, Inc., New York. This edition first
published in Great Britain by Kingfisher Books Ltd.,
a Grisewood & Dempsey Company, in 1989.

LIBRARY OF CONGRESS CATALOGING-IN-PUBLICATION DATA:
Salt, Jane
  See & say picture word book.
  SUMMARY: Illustrations and text introduce words
associated with school, home, play, shapes and sizes,
city life, transportation, and the beach.
  ISBN: 0-679-80099-9 (trade); 0-679-90099-3 (lib. bdg.)
  1. Vocabulary—Juvenile literature. [1. Vocabulary]
I. Pooley, Sarah, ill.   II. Title.   III. Title: See and say
picture word book.
PE1449.S2835 1989 428.1 89-3624

Manufactured in Spain   1 2 3 4 5 6 7 8 9 10

See & Say
Picture
Word Book

By Jane Salt

Illustrated by Sarah Pooley

Random House 🏠 New York

Introduction

Here are some ways you can help your child enjoy and learn with this book.

● Let your child spend as long as he or she likes on each page. Some pages will be looked at enthusiastically, others will be flicked over and returned to later.

● Talking and listening are very important. Help your child's conversational skills by discussing what the characters are doing.

● Prediction skills are essential for learning to read. Help encourage this by asking questions such as "What do you think that girl will do next?"

● Introduce your child to the printed word by pointing out some of the words you know she or he is interested in. Don't try to point out all the words at one time.

● Looking carefully plays an important part in the process of learning to read. Help your child develop visual skills by pointing out small details in the pictures.

● Give your child plenty of opportunity to browse through the book on his or her own. Private enjoyment of books is a very special and useful habit to foster.

This book is designed to be a fun way to learn. We hope you and your child will have many hours of enjoyment with it.

Contents

I like books!

Alphabet names

Anna

apple

Ben

Ouch!

ball

Corinne

comb

David

dancing

Natasha

Thanks!

Oscar

orange

nightie

Emily

elephant

foot

Freddy

teddy

saucepan

Pamela

quiet

Ssh!

rattle

Rory

Tina

Quentin

painting

Samantha

8   a b c d e f g h i j k l m

Look for the letter that begins your name.

Henry

hiding

Gloria

giggling

Isabelle

Whoops!

ink

James

Vicky

Beep!

jeans

umbrella

van

kitten

Katie

Leo

letter

Maylin

mud

Yolanda

yawning

wet

Umberto

William

Xavier

box

zoo

Zachary

The birthday party

Mom

Dad

Happy Birthday to you!

candle

Grandma

Happy Birthday to you!

Uncle

brother

cake

Grandpa

baby

sister

high chair

dog

10

balloons

cousin

Grandpa

Aunt

cat

Grandma

card

present

wrapping
paper

ribbon

11

Homes

Most homes always stay in the same place. But some homes can move around.

houseboat

mobile home

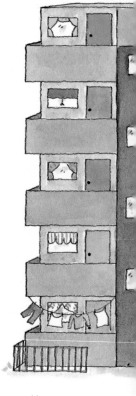

apartment house

Let's play house

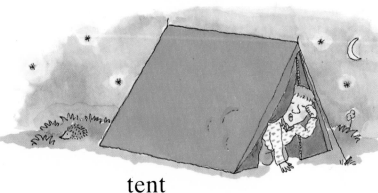

tent

clubhouse

Keep Out

cave

Hard rock cave

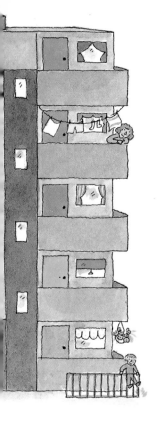

home

cottage

space house

nest

castle

13

The dollhouse – outside . . .

When you open the front door of
the dollhouse, you can see all
the rooms inside.

chimney

roof

curtain

window

window box
shade

garage

door

Teddy
is visiting
the doll-
house.

flowers

garden

gate

fence

. . . and inside

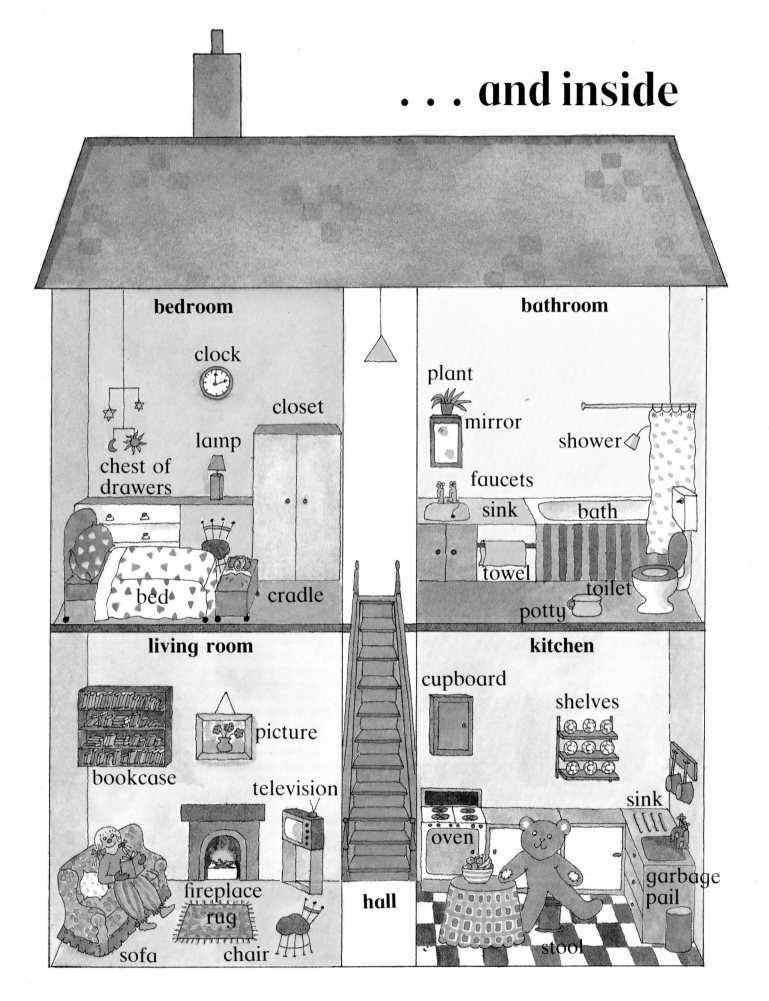

bedroom

clock

closet

lamp

chest of drawers

bed

cradle

bathroom

plant

mirror

shower

faucets

sink

bath

towel

toilet

potty

living room

picture

bookcase

television

fireplace

rug

sofa

chair

hall

kitchen

cupboard

shelves

sink

oven

garbage pail

stool

Time to eat

breakfast

lunch

Make a menu by writing down
your favorite kinds of food.

dinner

washing dishes

Menu
fish sticks
peas
salad
spaghetti
fruit

In the city

hospital

school

Out Patients

PUDDLEDUCK HOSPITAL

PARK ROAD SCHOOL

sign

fire engine

crosswalk

NOW SHOWING... "BABES-IN-THE-WOOD"

PALACE THEATER

Starring Ivy Leaf and Lily Bud

car

movie theater

traffic lights

PUDDLE DUCK PARK

park

synagogue

LAUNDROMAT

Maps tell us how to find the streets we want.

sidewalk

18

map

The checkup

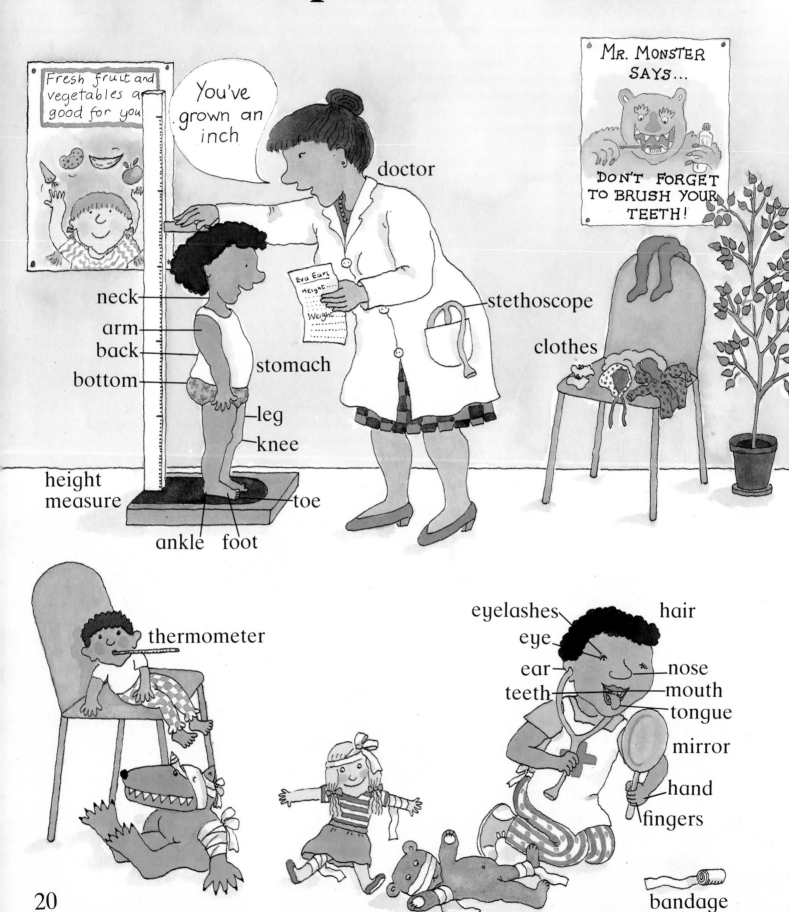

Fresh fruit and vegetables are good for you

You've grown an inch

doctor

Eva Earl
Height...
Weight...

stethoscope

clothes

MR. MONSTER SAYS...

DON'T FORGET TO BRUSH YOUR TEETH!

neck
arm
back
bottom
stomach
leg
knee

height measure

toe
ankle foot

thermometer

eyelashes hair
eye
ear nose
teeth mouth
tongue
mirror
hand
fingers

bandage

My Mommy by Tina

I love my baby sister by Emily

I am riding my bike Henry

My favorite food is fries by yolanda

peas in a pod by Anna

home corner

Apple tree by Zack

The very hungry Caterpillar

Bernard

Kate

Sana

In the Countryside

telephone

clay   pens
blocks   books
paint   paper
crayon   FELT PENS

dress-up box

nature corner

flowers

table

teacher

Messy!

chair

apron

wastebasket

paint

23

Clothes

closet

blouse

dress

coat

overalls

sweater

boots

sneakers

undershirt

pajamas

belt

slippers

skirt

pants

bathrobe

tights

T-shirt

socks

shoes

Colors

paintbrush

white   black   red   blue   green

24

Dress-up

Look for the different colors in the
picture.

yellow

pink

purple

orange

brown

gray

25

Workers

writer

secretary

Could you type this letter please!

firefighter

helmet

BUS

FIRE ENGINE

fire engine

Honest Josie's Garage "We'll fix it!"

The big red bus

hose

I can see the problem!

mechanics

ballet dancers

tutu

builder

27

Building words

sheet

level

drill

nails

clamp

box

hammer

MESSY MATT EMULSION

paint

Oops... too short!

string

plank of wood

paper

saw

scissors

workbench

screws

screwdriver

Glob's glue

glue

sticky cat

Vicky's shop

At the Supermarket

LIST

fish sticks
bananas
bread
potatoes
milk
yogurt
chicken
cat food
diapers
baked beans
orange juice

Dairy

yogurt

milk

cream

butter

orange juice

Can you help me find all these things on my shopping list?

basket

shopping cart

ENTRANCE

Fruit and Vegetables

Bakery

bread

assistant

cakes

potatoes

Weigh here

oranges bananas

Groceries

baked beans

chicken

fish sticks

Frozen foods

cash register

10

10.15

receipt

money

CHEAPIES Whole wheat cereal

Food is Fresh at CHEAPIES

diapers small

diapers large

diapers medium

diapers x-large

diapers x-large

purse

diapers

cat food

Food is Fresh at CHEAPIES SUPERMARKET

EXIT

31

Weather words

Whether the weather be hot,
or whether the weather be not,

snowflakes

skis

snowball

sled

icicle

ice

ice skates

wool
hat

coat

mittens

snowman

snow

snowshoes

snowy

hat

wind

kite

cloud

balloon

tree

daffodils

scarf

violets

crocuses

primroses

windy

We'll weather the weather, whatever the weather,

Whether we like it or not.

sunny

stormy

Puddleduck park

fence

merry-go-round

Seesaw, Margery Daw!

seesaw

I'm the King of the castle!

climbing fence

swing

slide

Watch me, Mom!

jump rope

buggy

bucket

sandbox

34

A picnic in the country

tractor

river

field

Bridle path

fence

Litter

Please shut the gate

Fresh fruit & veg

tree

bridge

rocks

frog

net

stream

grasshopper

dandelion

leaf

hill

branch

horse

bird's nest

Look!

binoculars

Bird guide

stepping stones

Splash

poppy

ants

37

At the beach

motorboat

sea gull
water-skier

swimmer

ocean

tube

water wings

Popsicle

swimming trunks

I'm eating a sand sandwich!

beach towel

blanket

suntan lotion

38

39

Things that go

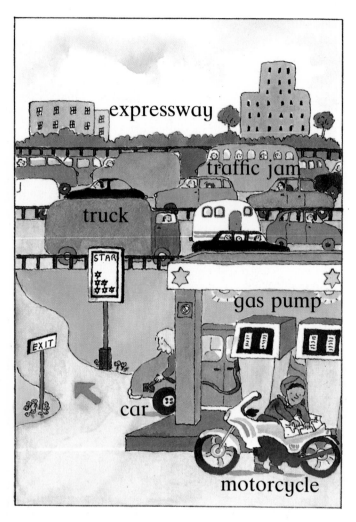

expressway

traffic jam

truck

gas pump

car

motorcycle

gas station

Platform 1

TOOTING

TOOTING

car

train

EXPRESS

engineer

ticket

engine

suitcase

platform

train station

engine

race-track

wheel

Whoops!

finish

start

racecar

40

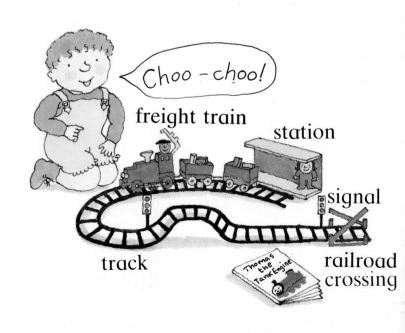

Choo-choo!

freight train

station

signal

track

Thomas the Tank Engine

railroad crossing

Cars, trains, boats, and airplanes are all different kinds of transportation.

airport

harbor

Animal friends

The animals went in two by two,
The elephant and the kangaroo.

panda

kangaroos

horses

dog

lions

leopards

penguin

I can't find the other tiger. Can you see it?

monkeys

seals

elephants

squirrels

rabbit

Noah's Ark

cats

snakes

tiger

ostriches

gorillas

deer

polar
bear

hippopotamus

sheep

duck

giraffe

crocodiles

foxes

43

Sizes . . .

The clown is tall,
but teddy is short.

1 yard

2 feet

1 foot

How tall are you?

high

low

tall

short

large

small

light

heavy

JIGSAW

circle

square

triangle

44

fat

thin

tiny

enormous

little

big

. . . and shapes

Look for these shapes in the picture.

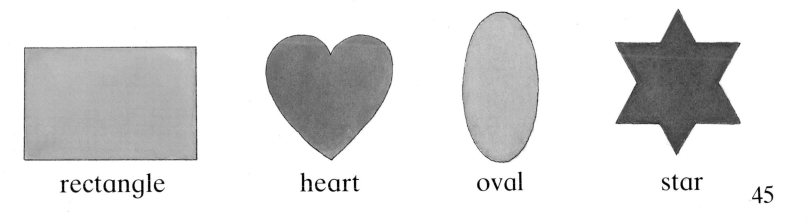

rectangle

heart

oval

star

45